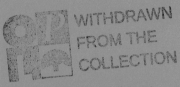

The Best Mother

By C. M. SURRISI
Illustrated by DIANE GOODE

ABRAMS BOOKS FOR YOUNG READERS · NEW YORK

The art in this book was made with pen and ink, watercolors, gouache, and pastels
on Arches watercolor paper.

Cataloging-in-Publication Data has been applied for and may be obtained from the Library of Congress.

ISBN 978-1-4197-2534-0

Text copyright © 2018 Cynthia Surrisi
Illustrations copyright © 2018 Diane Goode
Book design by Siobhán Gallagher

Printed and bound in China
10 9 8 7 6 5 4 3 2

Abrams Books for Young Readers are available at special discounts when purchased
in quantity for premiums and promotions as well as fundraising or educational use.
Special editions can also be created to specification. For details, contact
specialsales@abramsbooks.com or the address below.

ABRAMS The Art of Books
195 Broadway, New York, NY 10007
abramsbooks.com

For Magda, who is the best mother I know
—C.M.S.

For Peter
—D.G.

axine hated to get up in the morning. She didn't like to wash her face or brush her teeth or comb her hair. Maxine was sure a new mother would solve her problems.

At breakfast, Maxine's mother asked,
"What are you going to do today, Maxine?"
Maxine munched her toast.

"I'm going to get a new mother," she announced.

"Sounds like a good idea," said her old mother.

"I'm going to look in the park," Maxine said.

"And in the toy store. And at the zoo."

"You better take your sun hat. It will be hot and bright today," said her old mother.

"That is just the sort of thing I do not want my new mother to say," said Maxine.

But Maxine didn't know how to get to the park or the toy store or the zoo.

"Will you take me?" Maxine asked.

"I'd be happy to," said her old mother.

Maxine and her old mother arrived at the park.

"If you were my mother, would you make me pick up all my toys?" Maxine asked.

"You bet I would!"

Maxine thought, *Not that mother*.

"If you were my mother, would you let me bang a drum any time I want to?" Maxine asked.
"No banging drums, no tooting horns, no Miss Noisy, thank you very much."

Maxine thought, *Uh-oh. Not that mother.*

"If you were my mother, would you let me wear
my slippers in the snow?" Maxine asked.
"Ha, ha, ha. No."

Maxine thought, *Definitely not that mother.*

Maxine and her old mother arrived at the toy store.

"If you were my mother, would you buy me this rocket?"
Maxine asked.
"That rocket is too expensive."

Maxine thought, *Well, not that mother, either.*

"If you were my mother, would you buy me this mask?"
Maxine asked.

"Sorry. I do not approve of scary masks."

Maxine thought, *For sure, not that mother*.

"If you were my mother, would you—"
"Don't touch that. You'll break it."

Maxine thought, *Whoa, no way.*

Maxine and her old mother arrived at the zoo.

Maxine watched the animal mothers.
The monkey mother picked nits out of her monkey
baby's hair.

Maxine touched her hair.

The elephant mother sprayed her elephant baby with water.

Maxine put on her sun hat.

The giraffe mother licked the sore on her giraffe baby's neck.

Maxine looked at the bandage on her knee.

Maxine looked around for her old mother, the one who
invented the Toss-Your-Toys-in-the-Box game.

The mother who banged a
drum in her marching band,

and built a moonlight
snowman with her,
while wearing
their pajamas
and slippers
and parkas.

The mother who bought
her a telescope because
she promised to be
careful with it,

and played hide-and-seek
with her while wearing
monster masks.

Maxine found her old mother waiting with a balloon and a bag of hot peanuts, and she knew at that very moment that her old mother was the best new mother she could ever have.

"Hello," said Maxine's mother. "If you were my daughter, would you want this balloon?"

"I am your daughter," said Maxine.

"If you were my daughter, would you like these peanuts?"

"I AM YOUR DAUGHTER, MAMA!"

"If you were my daughter, would you want another mother?"

"Oh, Mama, don't be so silly," Maxine said.

"Oh, Maxine, I'm so glad."

"Mama?"

"Yes, Maxine?"

"Will it be hot and sunny tomorrow?"

"I don't know. Why do you ask?"

"If it is, I think we should wear our sun hats."